E
DeBr   De Brunhoff, Jean

Babar and the Ghost

A NOT

When y   giving ther   l as
giving   ing
Books   rced
with liv   read
fun, sa   that
acquirir   they
are beg   y're
written

Step   nely
simple   gest
readers   nore
difficul   ead-
ing lev   ater
reading   for
the incr

Chile   ling
Book   to
help c   _ter._
The   1ool
throug   2,
grades   tep
4—are   ove
throug   eps
over a   our
child

An easy-to-read version of *Babar and the Ghost*, published by Random House, Inc., in 1981. Copyright © 1981 by Laurent de Brunhoff.

Library of Congress Cataloging in Publication Data: Brunhoff, Laurent de. Babar and the ghost. (Step into reading. A Step 2 book) SUMMARY: The ghost of the Black Castle follows Babar and his family and friends back to Celesteville. [1. Ghosts—Fiction. 2. Elephants—Fiction] I. Title. II. Series. PZ7.B82843Baag   1986   [E]   85-11841   ISBN: 0-394-87908-2 (trade); 0-394-97908-7 (lib. bdg.)

Manufactured in the United States of America   13   14   15   16   17   18   19   20

STEP INTO READING is a trademark of Random House, Inc.

Step into Reading

BABAR
AND THE GHOST
An Easy-to-Read Version

By Laurent de Brunhoff

A Step 2 Book

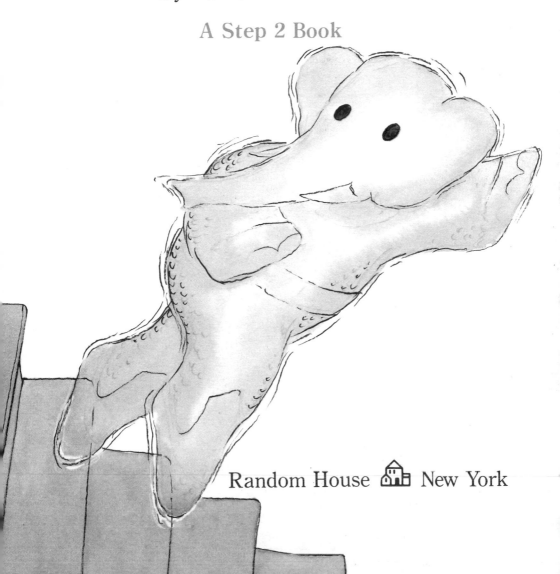

Random House New York

Babar and his family
were going to Black Castle.
They were going
to have a picnic there.
The children were very excited.

4

"We will miss you!"

cried the children.

"I will miss you too,"

said Baron Bardula.

"But you can come visit me."

Then, as the children waved good-bye,

the ghost flew off to Black Castle.

That night at dinner
the children looked so sad.
"It is going to be sunny
and hot all week,"
Babar told them.
"Do you want to go
on another hike to Black Castle?"

"Yes! Yes!"

cried all the children.

They could visit the ghost very soon!

"But there will be no more

talk about ghosts,"

Babar said to the children.

"Because we all know—"

"Yes! Yes! We know!"
shouted the children.
"THERE IS NO SUCH THING
AS A GHOST!"
Babar just smiled.

"We want to see the ghost!"

they shouted.

"We want to see the ghost

of Black Castle."

"There is no such thing
as a ghost,"
King Babar said.
"Of course not,"
said Queen Celeste.
"Now, come help me
with the picnic lunch."

Pom, Flora, and Alexander
spread out a blanket.
Their cousin Arthur
got out the food.
Zephir the monkey
put out plates and cups.
Everyone was very hungry.

But soon dark clouds
filled the sky.
And big drops of rain
began to fall.
"A storm!" said Babar.
Everyone ran to the castle.

8

9

The castle was old and dark.

All at once something brushed

past Zephir's face.

"Oh!" shouted Zephir.

"What was that?"

"It was just a bat,"

Babar told him.

Babar made a fire.
"We will stay here
until the rain stops,"
said Babar.
"Good!" said Arthur.
"Let's see what's here."

The children ran all over the castle.

They ran up the stairs.

They ran down the stairs.

The old floors creaked.

"Oooh! A ghost! A ghost!"

the children shouted, and laughed.

Pom was running very fast.

He bumped into a suit of armor.

Crash!

Pom fell down.

So did the armor.

"Get up!" said the children.

But it was not Pom

who got up.

It was the suit of armor!

It pulled open its helmet.

A ghost poked its head out.

A real ghost!

The ghost flew out.

"Hello!" it said.

"I am Baron Bardula."

The children were

too scared to move.

16

"Please do not be scared,"

said the ghost.

"I am a nice ghost.

Let me show you around my castle."

The children looked at the ghost.

He really did not seem very scary.

The children followed the ghost.

He told them that long ago

he had been a brave knight.

"I fought many dragons,"

he said.

"But now I am a ghost. See!"

18

All of a sudden

Baron Bardula was gone.

Then he was back.

He walked right through the wall.

What a good trick!

The children were having lots of fun.

Then they heard Babar call,

"Children! Where are you?

The rain has stopped.

We can go home now."

"I wish you did not have to go,"

the ghost said sadly.

"Why don't you come home with us?"

said Arthur.

"That does sound like fun,"

said the ghost.

"But only you will see me.

The grownups will not know I am around."

Everybody laughed.

What fun it was going to be!

A little later

everybody left the castle.

So did the ghost.

The very next morning

the fun began.

Celeste was in the garden.

"Be a nice ghost,"

Zephir whispered to the baron.

"Give the queen some lemonade."

Suddenly the pitcher went
up, up, up.
It filled the glass
with lemonade.

"Did you see that, Zephir?"

cried Celeste.

Zephir did not answer.

He was laughing too hard.

A little later

Babar was planting flowers.

Arthur was helping him.

All at once

they heard the lawn mower.

It was running by itself.

Putt, putt, putt.

It went right through the flowers!

Arthur started to laugh.

"That is not funny,"

said Babar.

"I think Zephir did that."

"No, he did not," said Arthur.

And he laughed again.

That night there was music.
Suddenly a loud screech
came from the saxophone!

"Who did that?" shouted Babar.
The children knew
but they did not say!

29

The children loved the ghost.

They wanted him to stay forever.

The most fun of all

was playing hide-and-seek.

The children looked under the bed.

They looked
in the closet.

They looked behind the curtains.
"Baron, Baron, where are you?"
they called.

At last they found him.

He was in a chest,

folded up like a sheet.

The children laughed and laughed.

Just then the door flew open.

"Who were you talking to?"

asked Babar.

"Nobody. We are just playing,"

said the children.

"Hmmm," said Babar.

"Something strange is going on."

34

Babar went for a walk.

He thought and thought

about all the strange tricks.

Suddenly horns began honking.

Cars bumped into each other.

Everyone began shouting.

Babar looked up.

A red car was racing down the street.

The car had no driver!

The children saw the red car too.

"There is the ghost!"

Alexander cried.

The red car just missed a tree.

Then it came to a stop.

The children ran to the car.

The ghost was shaking all over.

"I have never driven a car before,"

he said in a scared voice.

"And I never want to drive one again.

I want to go back to the castle."

"Please stay,"

Flora said.

"You are such a nice ghost."

Babar ran over to the children.

He heard

what Flora had said.

Ghost!

Babar saw no ghost.

Babar was mad.

He shouted,

"Ghost, if you are there,

hear me!

I have had enough of

your tricks.

You must leave NOW."

And with that
Babar turned
and left.

"Your father is right,"

   the ghost said to the children.

"I have had a very good time

   with all of you.

But this busy life

   is too much for an old ghost like me.

It is time for me to go home."